A WEEK PAST FOREVER

By Cynthia DiLaura Devore, M.D.

Published by Abdo & Daughters, 4940 Viking Drive, Suite 622, Edina, Minnesota 55435.

Library bound edition distributed by Rockbottom Books, Pentagon Towers, P.O. Box 36036, Minneapolis, Minnesota 55435.

Edited by Julie Berg

LIBRARY OF CONGRESS CATALOGING-IN-PUBLICATION DATA

Devore, Cynthia DiLaura, 1947-
   A week past forever / written by Cynthia DiLaura Devore.
      p. cm. -- (Children of courage)
   Summary: As they walk along the beach. Nita and her favorite uncle, who is dying of AIDS, talk about the importance of taking care of oneself by making careful choices in life and how love continues long after death. Includes how-to's.
      ISBN 1-56239-246-8
      [1. AIDS (Disease) -- Fiction. 2. Uncles -- Fiction. 3. Choice -- Fiction. 4. Death -- Fiction.] I. Title. II. Series: Devore, Cynthia DiLaura. 1947-   Children of courage.
   PZ7.D4993We   1993
   [Fic}--dc20
                                      93-7722
                                        CIP
                                        AC

Terminal illness imparts a sense of urgency on the individual to share with children values and philosophies of her/his own. The AIDS epidemic has taken many lives and will likely take many more before a cure is found. Whether it is AIDS or any other terminal illness, A WEEK PAST FOREVER is a useful story to build a child's understanding in the importance of taking care of oneself wholly as well as coping with the impending loss of a loved one. It follows a man and his niece on an enchanted walk of love, interweaving reality with fantasy in a celebration of life.

It was a magnificent day. The sky was just about as blue as Paolos had ever remembered. The ocean air smelled sweet and clean. A warm breeze blew gently over the water causing the waves to roll in. The sound of the waves was rhythmic and soothing. The world seemed glorious to him now. All his senses were alive. He sat comfortably in a wooden chair near the water and shifted his bare feet in the warm sand. "This is a perfect day for a celebration," he spoke aloud to no one. "A celebration for me and my little Nita on our Enchanted Beach."

"Uncle Paolos," he heard his niece call as she came running toward him. She was carrying a small bag. Her parents waved from afar and drove off to allow Nita to spend some private time with her favorite Uncle Paolos.

"Nita, I have been waiting for you," he called. He opened his arms to catch her.

There was so much he wanted to tell his darling Nita. He knew the virus that was destroying his body would no longer slow down its deadly course. Time was so precious. So he chose here and now to tell her what he had to say. In this magical place, the rest of the world disappeared in imaginary play. They were rulers of their Enchanted Beach, a Kingdom for a kind king and a little princess.

"King Paolos, I bring you gifts," she said curtsying like a princess. She opened the bag to reveal with pride the slightly crumbled chocolate chip cookies.

"Splendid, fair princess," he said in his king's voice. He took a cookie from the bag and bit into it as if it were a rare delicacy. "Ummm, DE-licious," he said pausing, "but not as delicious as you." He pretended to take a bite from her neck, and she giggled.

"Princess Nita, I could eat your whole bag of cookies," he said. "There must be dozens in there, and that's an awful lot." His voice was playfully sing-song, as he shook his pointer finger at her nose, the way he always did when he said, "that's an awful lot" to her.

She laughed and grabbed his finger. Then she hugged him tightly.

Nita and Paolos were the best of friends. They had talked many times during the past year about his illness. She knew Paolos had AIDS. They both knew he would not live much longer. He wanted her to learn from his mistakes, as much as a six-year-old child could grasp. That was why he had arranged to have this meeting.

"Uncle Paolos," she asked suddenly and with the honesty of a secure child, "will you be able to see me after you die?"

Startled by her openness he answered, "I don't know, my princess. I only know that I will always be in your heart even if you cannot see me." He kissed her cheek and held her close to him. "I must tell you some important things, Nita. You must be very big and very smart as you listen to what I say."

She sat on the soft sand at his feet. "I'll try," she promised.

He leaned his frail body back in the chair, looked right in her eyes and spoke slowly and deliberately.

"Nita, life is like our Enchanted Beach, where you and I walk on soft sand at the edge of the water."

She listened intently.

"If you step carefully and make each step you take as important as the last, your footing will be steady and safe," he said. "Do you understand?"

"A little," she answered.

"But if you walk carelessly or recklessly, you are taking the chance that your next step might cause you to lose your balance," he continued.

"And then you would fall right into the water. Right, Uncle Paolos?" She climbed onto his thin lap.

"Yes, Nita, exactly. Then you might get hurt or drown."

"Or eaten by a shark, right?" she said, finishing his thought.

"Or eaten by a shark, Nita," he said with a smile. "So, in life you must make every step you take count."

"Do you mean like this?" she asked as she stood up and walked stiffly, placing her bare feet cautiously one in front of the other.

Paolos laughed. "Well, not exactly, my little bunny." He slowly rose to join her. They splashed water as they walked holding hands down the empty beach. The sun's reflection shimmered color on the water.

"What I mean is that everything you do in life matters," he continued. "Everything you do has a consequence. That means that something good will come of every wise choice, and something bad might happen from every poor choice. Does that make sense to you?" he asked as they stopped beneath a tree to cool off in the shade.

"Yes," she said.

"Every risk you take, even once, can be dangerous, Nita. You must chose your risks carefully in life. Take a risk only if it seems like something really worth doing. I do not want you to get hurt acting recklessly or foolishly. Whatever choices you make must be made with dignity and respect for yourself, your body, and your brain. Do you understand?" They left the shade of the tree and walked back to the water's edge to watch the crab scurrying about.

"I think so," she replied. "I think it means that everything I do matters. If I have good behavior, good things will happen. And if I have bad behavior, bad things will happen."

"Well, you're almost right," he said. "There are some things we cannot control. There are some things we can control, like our choices. If we make bad choices, bad things might happen. And if we make good choices, good things might happen. Does that make sense, Nita?"

"You mean that even if there is something I really, really, really want to do, you want me to stop and think about what might happen if I do it," she said. "If it might be something bad, you do not want me to do it unless I have a good chance of not getting into trouble."

"Or hurting yourself," he added. "Yes, my princess, you understand so well."

They walked a short distance more down the beach. They came to a long stump of gray twisted driftwood, smoothed by the water and dried by the warm sun. It was their imaginary throne.

"Uncle Paolos, if everything I do matters, does that mean I'm very special?" she asked. They sat on their throne. She leaned her head against his bony arm. They loved each other so much.

"Yes, dearest Nita, you are very special," he said. "There is no one else in this world like you. That is why you must always be your own person. Believe in yourself. Remember who you are. Do not let others make you do something you know is not safe. Choose carefully and thoughtfully. Treat your body and brain with care and respect, because you are so special."

They sat there quietly for a moment watching the sunset. They each knew that their simple walk had been a wonderful celebration of life. Their love spoke through the silence.

"Nita, will you always love me even after I have died?" He sounded more like the child now, needing support.

She stood up in front of him, her head held high, and her hands on her hips as if she were a princess in charge of the moment. "King Paolos of the Enchanted Beach," she said with a tone of reassurance only this child could give this man, "do you really want to know how long I will love you?"

"Yes, Princess Nita, please make your decree," he replied in his most kingly voice. Though tired, he sat upright and made an effort to look like a king.

"I, Princess Nita, the wisest princess in all the land, do hereby decree that I will love King Paolos for one week past forever." Then she leaned forward, put up her pointer finger to touch his nose and sang, "And that's an awful lot."

He smiled and hugged her. "You are right, Princess Nita, that *is* an awful lot." And nothing more needed to be said.